ATTACK
of the
GIANT Baby!

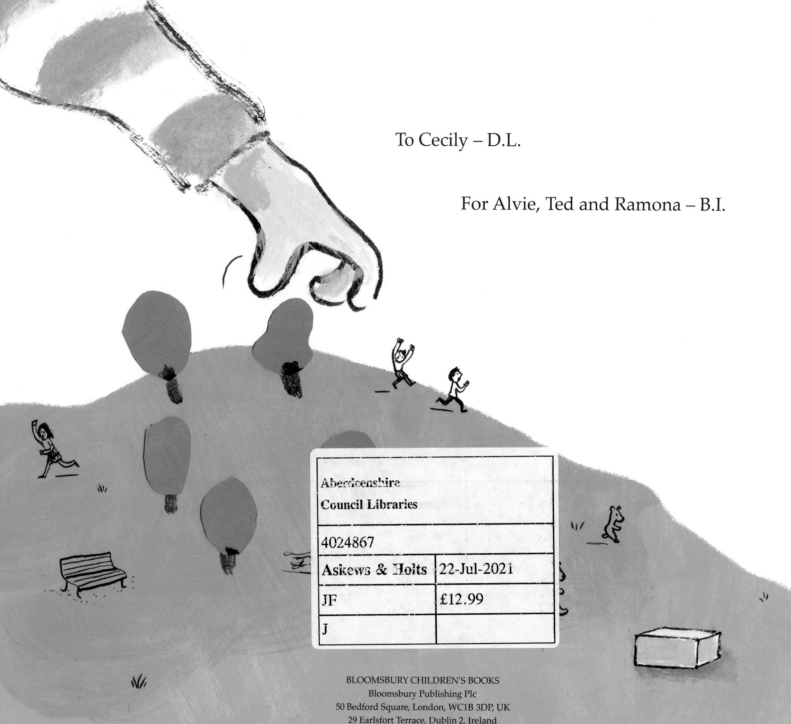

To Cecily – D.L.

For Alvie, Ted and Ramona – B.I.

BLOOMSBURY CHILDREN'S BOOKS
Bloomsbury Publishing Plc
50 Bedford Square, London, WC1B 3DP, UK
29 Earlsfort Terrace, Dublin 2, Ireland

BLOOMSBURY, BLOOMSBURY CHILDREN'S BOOKS and the Diana logo are trademarks of Bloomsbury Publishing Plc
First published in Great Britain 2021 by Bloomsbury Publishing Plc

Text copyright © David Lucas, 2021
Illustrations copyright © Bruce Ingman, 2021

David Lucas and Bruce Ingman have asserted their rights under the Copyright, Designs and Patents Act, 1988,
to be identified as the Author and Illustrator of this work

A catalogue record for this book is available from the British Library

ISBN 978 1 4088 9985 4 (HB)
ISBN 978 1 4088 9986 1 (eBook)

1 3 5 7 9 10 8 6 4 2

Printed and bound in China by Leo Paper Products, Heshan, Guangdong

To find out more about our authors and books visit www.bloomsbury.com and sign up for our newsletters

ATTACK
of the
GIANT Baby!

Written by

David Lucas

Illustrated by

Bruce Ingman

BLOOMSBURY
CHILDREN'S BOOKS
LONDON OXFORD NEW YORK NEW DELHI SYDNEY

The King and Queen

were having breakfast, when a royal
messenger burst in.

"A Giant Baby!" he gasped.

"Destroying everything
in its path."

The King looked out from the battlements.
"Our kingdom is in peril!" he cried.

"Save us!" wailed
the Queen

"Save us!" squealed
the courtiers.

"He's just a **baby**," said
the Princess, but no one
listened to her.

Giant Baby **toppled** the tallest mountains.

Giant Baby **trampled** the forest.

Giant Baby
flattened
houses
and
bridges.

The people of the kingdom were
running for their **lives**.

"Do something!" yelled the Queen.

"Do something!" yelled the courtiers.

"Do something!" yelled the King.

The Queen
rolled her eyes.

"Oh,
you want ME
to do something,"
said the King. "But WHAT?"

"He's just a baby," said the Princess,
but no one listened to her.

Giant Baby sat down
p l o p!
on the
train station.

Giant Baby
S H O O K
all the passengers
out of a
double-decker
bus.

The King summoned his advisers.

The King banged the table.
"We need a plan!"
he said.

"This calls for
expert diplomacy!"
said his advisers.

"Delicate
negotiations!"

"An international
PEACE
conference . . ."

"He's just a baby,"
said the Princess, but no one
listened to her.

Giant Baby
CRASHED
through the
castle wall.

Giant Baby stood at the
castle gate.

The King looked very serious indeed.

"My friends," he said. "We **must** defend ourselves."

"He's just a **baby**," said the Princess, but no one listened to her.

"Send out my **knights** in **shining armour!**" said the King.

But the knights in shining armour
were NO match for Giant Baby.

"Send in
the Airforce!"
said the King.

But the Royal Airforce was NO match for Giant Baby.

It worked!

Giant Baby had STOPPED.

Giant Baby was cuddling
the Monster-sized Bear.

"Three cheers for Bear!"
cried the King.

Oh. Giant Baby DIDN'T want to cuddle Bear anymore.

Giant Baby just
KNOCKED
Bear aside.

"We're doomed!"
wailed the Queen.

"We're doomed!"
wailed the courtiers.

"He's just a baby," said the Princess,
but no one listened to her.

"Not so fast, Giant Baby!" said the King.
"We're NOT done yet!"

And
from
the
deepest,
DARKEST dungeon
he summoned the
Really SCARY
Skeleton Dragon
with the Spiky Tail
and
Flashing Eyes!"

But even the Really SCARY Skeleton Dragon with the Spiky Tail
and Flashing Eyes was NO MATCH for Giant Baby.

The castle was in ruins.

"My beautiful home!"
sobbed the Queen.

"We have only one option left!" said the King.
He looked up at Giant Baby. He was utterly defeated.
"Take my crown! My gold. My jewels.
But I beg you, leave us be!"

Giant Baby
shook his head . . .

Giant Baby
KNOCKED
the King, the Queen,
the royal advisers
and all the courtiers
FLAT.

The Princess stood alone.
She wasn't afraid.

"He's just a baby,"
she said.

She spoke to Giant Baby.
"Where's your Mummy?"

Giant Baby didn't know.
Giant Baby began to cry.

"Come on," said the Princess, gently.
"Let's find her."

Mummy was in the kitchen.

"I think **Baby** is **hungry** now," said the Princess.

"So *there* you are!" said Mummy.
"Supper's ready."

And while **Giant Baby** had his supper,
his big sister **tidied up**
her **TOY** kingdom.

"We were lucky to escape with our lives!" said the King.

"But you were so brave!" said the Queen.

The Princess smiled.

And life across the kingdom
got back to normal.

Until . . .

A royal messenger burst in!